Sir Arthur Conan Doyle's

The Adventure of the Three Students

Adapted by: Vincent Goodwin

Illustrated by: Ben Dunn

visit us at
www.abdopublishing.com

Published by Magic Wagon, a division of the ABDO Group, PO Box 398166, Minneapolis, MN, 55439.

Printed in the United States of America, North Mankato, Minnesota.
022012
092012
This book contains at least 10% recycled materials.

Written by Sir Arthur Conan Doyle
Adapted by Vincent Goodwin
Illustrated by Ben Dunn
Colored by Robby Bevard
Lettered by Doug Dlin
Edited by Stephanie Hedlund and Rochelle Baltzer
Interior layout by Antarctic Press
Cover art by Ben Dunn
Cover design by Abbey Fitzgerald

Library of Congress Cataloging-in-Publication Data

Goodwin, Vincent.
Sir Arthur Conan Doyle's The adventure of the three students / adapted by Vincent Goodwin ; illustrated by Ben Dunn.
p. cm. -- (The graphic novel adventures of Sherlock Holmes)
Summary: Retold in graphic novel form, Sherlock Holmes solves the mystery of who cheated and copied the Greek portion of an important examination.
ISBN 978-1-61641-895-3
1. Doyle, Arthur Conan, Sir, 1859-1930. Adventure of the three students--Adaptations. 2. Holmes, Sherlock (Fictitious character)--Comic books, strips, etc. 3. Holmes, Sherlock (Fictitious character)--Juvenile fiction. 4. Graphic novels. [1. Graphic novels. 2. Doyle, Arthur Conan, Sir, 1859-1930. Adventure of the three students--Adaptations. 3. Mystery and detective stories.] I. Dunn, Ben, ill. II. Doyle, Arthur Conan, Sir, 1859-1930. Adventure of the three students. III. Title. IV. Title: Adventure of the three students. V. Series: Goodwin, Vincent. Graphic novel adventures of Sherlock Holmes.
PZ7.7.G66Siu 2012
741.5'973--dc23

2011052264

Table of Contents

Cast

Sherlock Holmes

Dr. John Watson

Gilchrist

Daulat Ras

Miles McLaren

Professor Soames

Bannister

The Adventure of the Three Students
I'VE GOT IT, WATSON!

THESE WRITINGS AREN'T FROM THE TIME OF RAMSES...
THAT MEANS--

EXCUSE ME, MR. HOLMES?
I'M BUSY.

I NEED YOUR HELP. WE'VE HAD A PAINFUL INCIDENT AT THE UNIVERSITY. ONLY SOMEONE OF YOUR EXPERTISE COULD HELP SOLVE IT.
CALL THE POLICE. WATSON AND I ARE QUITE BUSY RIGHT NOW.

NO, NO, MY DEAR SIR. THIS IS ONE OF THOSE CASES WHERE I WOULD LIKE TO AVOID SCANDAL. AND YOUR DISCRETION IS WELL-KNOWN.

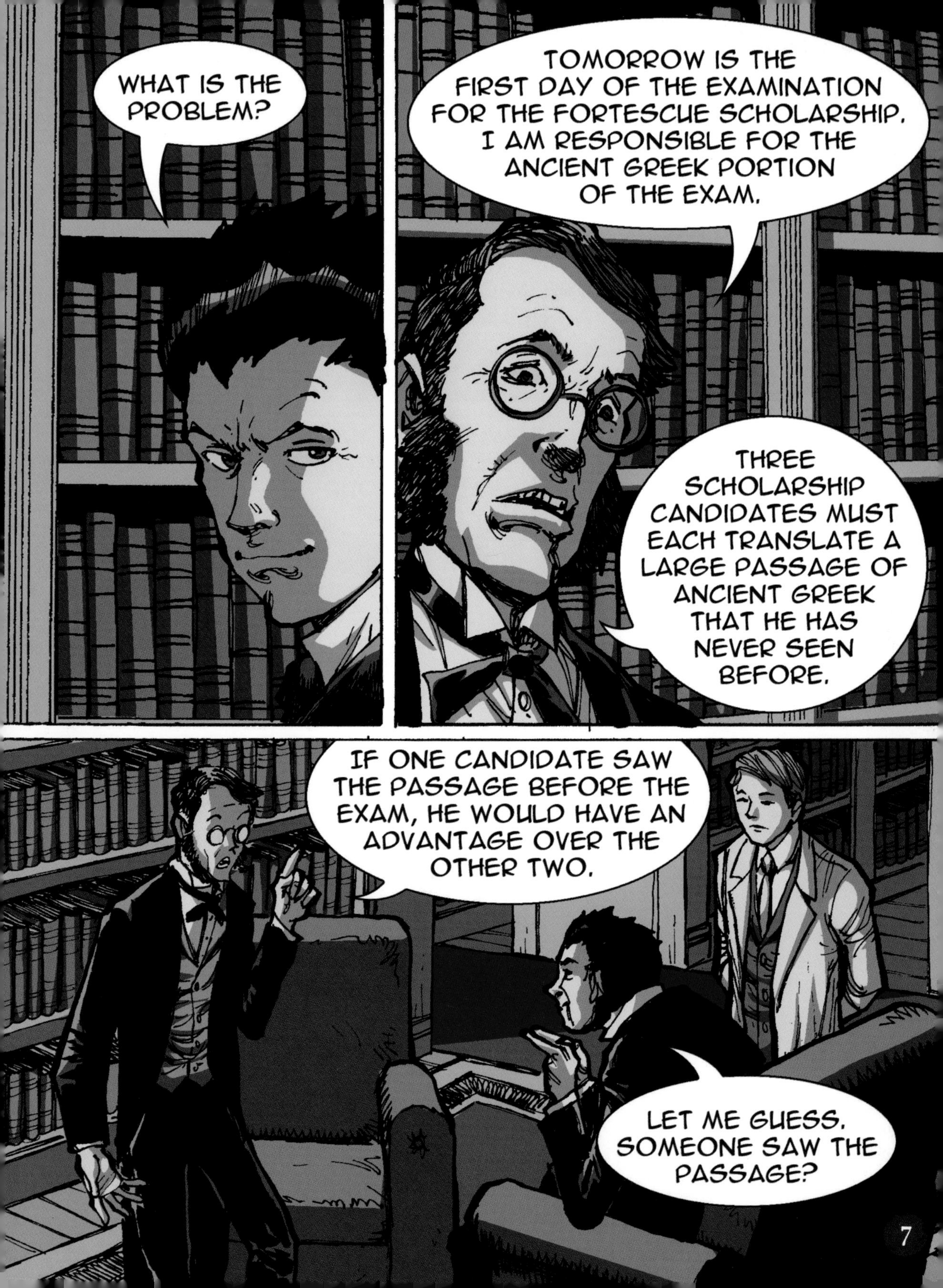
WHAT IS THE PROBLEM?
TOMORROW IS THE FIRST DAY OF THE EXAMINATION FOR THE FORTESCUE SCHOLARSHIP. I AM RESPONSIBLE FOR THE ANCIENT GREEK PORTION OF THE EXAM.
THREE SCHOLARSHIP CANDIDATES MUST EACH TRANSLATE A LARGE PASSAGE OF ANCIENT GREEK THAT HE HAS NEVER SEEN BEFORE.
IF ONE CANDIDATE SAW THE PASSAGE BEFORE THE EXAM, HE WOULD HAVE AN ADVANTAGE OVER THE OTHER TWO.
LET ME GUESS. SOMEONE SAW THE PASSAGE?

A FRIEND ASKED ME TO GO FOR TEA. I LEFT THE PASSAGE ON MY DESK, LOCKED MY OFFICE, AND WENT. I WAS GONE ABOUT AN HOUR.

"WHEN I CAME BACK, THERE WAS A KEY IN MY DOOR. BUT *MY* KEY WAS IN MY POCKET."

WHO ELSE HAS A COPY OF THE KEY TO YOUR OFFICE?
JUST MY SERVANT, BANNISTER. HE SAID HE ENTERED MY ROOM TO KNOW IF I WANTED TEA AND CARELESSLY LEFT THE KEY IN THE HOLE.

NORMALLY,
THIS WOULD BE A SMALL
MATTER. BUT ON THIS DAY,
SOMEBODY BROKE INTO
MY OFFICE.

YOU WANT
TO CHECK IT
OUT?
WHY
NOT?

Sherlock Holmes's guide to the crime scene…
THE MOMENT I LOOKED AT MY DESK, I KNEW SOMEBODY HAD GONE THROUGH MY PAPERS.
THE PASSAGE WAS THREE PAGES LONG. I HAD LEFT THEM ALL TOGETHER, BUT THEY WERE STREWN ABOUT THE ROOM.
Page 2 is on the floor.
Page 3 is on the windowsill.

THE MAN MUST HAVE COPIED THE PAPERS OVER HERE. THAT WAY HE COULD SEE IF YOU WERE COMING.
Page 1 is located on the desk, where all three pages should have been.

MAYBE YOUR MAN BANNISTER HAD SOMETHING TO DO WITH THE BREAK-IN?
BANNISTER HAS WORKED FOR ME FOR TEN YEARS. HIS HONESTY IS NOT IN QUESTION. BUT YES, I DID ASK HIM, AND HE SAID HE HAS NO IDEA.

HE WAS QUITE UPSET ABOUT IT. HE NEARLY COLLAPSED IN THAT CHAIR THERE.

SO MAYBE SOMEONE SAW THE KEY IN THE DOOR AND WENT TO LOOK AT THE PAPERS.
THAT'S EXACTLY WHAT I WAS THINKING. THE SCHOLARSHIP IS QUITE LARGE.
ARE THERE ANY MORE CLUES?

Sherlock Holmes's guide to the crime scene, continued…
IT LOOKS LIKE THE RASCAL WAS COPYING THE PAPER IN A HURRY AND BROKE HIS PENCIL. THEN, HE SHARPENED IT AGAIN.
A BLUE PENCIL.
YES, WITH SILVER LETTERING IN THE SHAVINGS.
Broken pencil lead and pencil shavings are found on the windowsill.
I JUST GOT THIS DESK LAST WEEK. AND THIS CUT WAS NOT HERE BEFORE LUNCH.
ΑΒΓΔΕ
ΖΗΘΚ
ΛΜΝΞ
ΠΡΣΤΥ
ΦΧΨΩ
A deep scratch can be seen in the desk.
IT LOOKS LIKE THE CULPRIT TRACKED IN CLAY OR SOME TYPE OF MUD.
Black clay is found on the carpet.

YOU MUST FIND OUT WHO DID THIS.
CAN YOU GET A NEW GREEK PASSAGE?

NO, WATSON, THEN PEOPLE WOULD ASK WHY THE EXAM WAS POSTPONED.
THAT WOULD BRING LIGHT TO THIS SCANDAL, WHICH I'M SURE THIS UNIVERSITY DOES NOT NEED.
SO YOU UNDERSTAND MY DILEMMA.

YES, I DO. MR. SOAMES, I WILL DO WHAT I CAN.

WHERE DOES THAT DOOR LEAD?
TO MY BEDROOM.
DO YOU MIND IF I TAKE A LOOK?
I LOOKED IN THERE AFTER I CAME IN, BUT GO AHEAD.

MR. SOAMES, IT SEEMS YOUR VISITOR ALSO LEFT TRACES IN YOUR BEDROOM.
WHAT COULD HE HAVE WANTED THERE?
CLEARLY HE NEEDED TO HIDE.

YOU MEAN THE WHOLE TIME I WAS TALKING TO BANNISTER IN MY OFFICE, WE HAD THIS MAN TRAPPED?
IT APPEARS THAT WAY.

WHO ARE THE THREE STUDENTS COMPETING FOR THE SCHOLARSHIP?

"THE FIRST IS GILCHRIST. HE DOES TRACK AND FIELD FOR THE UNIVERSITY. THE FAMILY FELL ON HARD TIMES, BUT THE BOY IS A GOOD STUDENT."

"THE SECOND IS DAULAT RAS. HE'S AN INDIAN STUDENT. HE IS VERY SMART, ALTHOUGH ANCIENT GREEK IS HIS WEAKEST SUBJECT."

"THE LAST IS MILES MCLAREN. HE'S BRILLIANT TOO, BUT UNDISCIPLINED. HE ONLY STUDIES WHEN HE WANTS TO. HE'S BEEN SEEN STRESSING ABOUT THE EXAM."

DID ANYONE VISIT YOUR OFFICE AFTER YOU DISCOVERED THE SCENE?
DAULAT RAS CAME BY.

DID HE SEE THE GREEK PASSAGE ON YOUR DESK?
NO, IT WAS ROLLED UP.

DID ANYONE KNOW THE PASSAGE WAS IN YOUR OFFICE?
NO. NOT EVEN BANNISTER.
INTERESTING. LET'S GO TALK TO BANNISTER.

I UNDERSTAND THAT YOU LEFT YOUR KEY IN THE DOOR?
YES, SIR.
WAS IT NOT VERY EXTRAORDINARY THAT YOU SHOULD DO THIS ON THE VERY DAY WHEN THERE WERE THESE PAPERS INSIDE?
I HAVE DONE THE SAME THING AT OTHER TIMES. I'M SURE YOU'VE DONE IT ONCE OR TWICE YOURSELF.
WHEN DID YOU ENTER MR. SOAMES'S OFFICE?
IT WAS AT HALF PAST FOUR.
HOW LONG WERE YOU IN THERE?
JUST FOR A MOMENT. I WITHDREW WHEN I SAW HE WASN'T THERE.

DID YOU LOOK AT THE PAPERS ON THE TABLE?
CERTAINLY NOT, SIR. I LEFT IMMEDIATELY.

WHEN MR. SOAMES TOLD YOU ABOUT THE BREAK-IN, HE SAID YOU WERE VERY UPSET.
I NEARLY FAINTED! SUCH A THING HAS NEVER HAPPENED DURING THE MANY YEARS I HAVE BEEN HERE.

WHERE WERE YOU WHEN HE TOLD YOU?
NEAR THE DOOR.

AND YOU WENT TO THE CHAIR ACROSS THE ROOM?
I DON'T KNOW, SIR. IT DIDN'T MATTER TO ME WHERE I SAT.
INTRIGUING!
WHAT HAPPENED AFTER THAT?
MR. SOAMES WENT INTO THE OTHER ROOM TO INVESTIGATE. THEN HE WENT TO GO FIND YOU, I GUESS.
YOU STAYED IN THE CHAIR WHEN YOUR MASTER LEFT?
ONLY FOR A MINUTE OR SO. THEN I LOCKED THE DOOR AND WENT TO MY ROOM.

DO YOU SUSPECT BANNISTER?
I DON'T KNOW. I'D LIKE TO TALK TO THE STUDENTS. IS THAT POSSIBLE?
NOT A PROBLEM AT ALL. RIGHT THIS WAY.

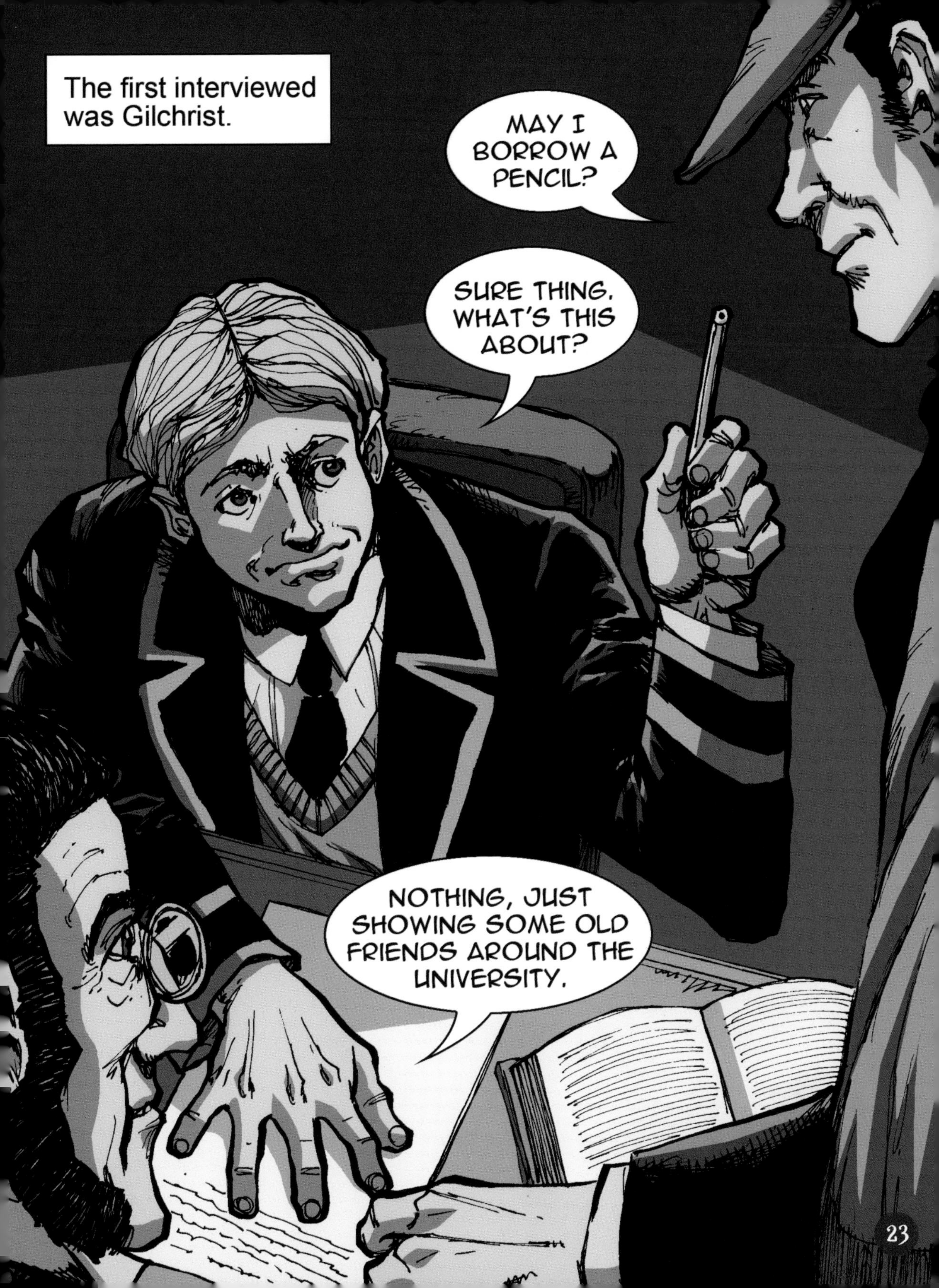
The first interviewed was Gilchrist.
MAY I BORROW A PENCIL?
SURE THING. WHAT'S THIS ABOUT?
NOTHING, JUST SHOWING SOME OLD FRIENDS AROUND THE UNIVERSITY.

Next they visited Ras.
MAY I BORROW A PENCIL?
THERE'S ONE OVER THERE. CAN YOU PLEASE BE QUIET? I'M TRYING TO STUDY.

Finally, they tried to see McLaren.
MAY I BORROW A PENCIL?
YOU CAN SCRAM! THAT'S WHAT YOU CAN DO!

DON'T YOU REALIZE THE TEST IS TOMORROW?!
HE IS A RUDE FELLOW. AND UNDER THE CIRCUMSTANCES, THAT MAKES ME RATHER SUSPICIOUS.
HOW TALL IS MR. MCLAREN?
I DON'T KNOW.
WHEN MR. HOLMES ASKS A QUESTION, IT'S USUALLY VERY IMPORTANT.
HE'S 5 FOOT 6, MAYBE?
THANK YOU. GOOD NIGHT.
I WILL DROP BY IN THE MORNING TO CHAT THE MATTER OVER. I MIGHT HAVE EVEN FIGURED IT OUT.

WELL, WATSON, WHAT DO YOU THINK OF IT?

IT MUST BE ONE OF YOUR THREE MEN. I SAY THE FOUL-MOUTHED FELLOW. THE INDIAN WAS ALSO SUSPICIOUS, THOUGH.

YOU KNOW WHO TROUBLES ME? THE SERVANT, BANNISTER. WHAT'S HIS GAME?
HE STRUCK ME AS BEING A PERFECTLY HONEST MAN.
SAME HERE. THAT'S THE PUZZLING PART.

DUNN & SON
OKS
STAT
LET'S STOP IN.

DO YOU SELL BLUE PENCILS WITH SILVER LETTERING?
YES, IT'S OUR MOST POPULAR BRAND. WE HAVE IT RIGHT HERE.
DRAT.
PENCILS 2p
PENCILS

IT APPEARS OUR BEST AND ONLY CLUE MEANS NOTHING.
I WAS HOPING THAT IT WOULD BE AN UNCOMMON PENCIL THAT ONLY ONE OF THE THREE STUDENTS PURCHASED.
HAVE YOU ANYTHING POSITIVE TO TELL SOAMES?
I DO NOT.

The next morning…

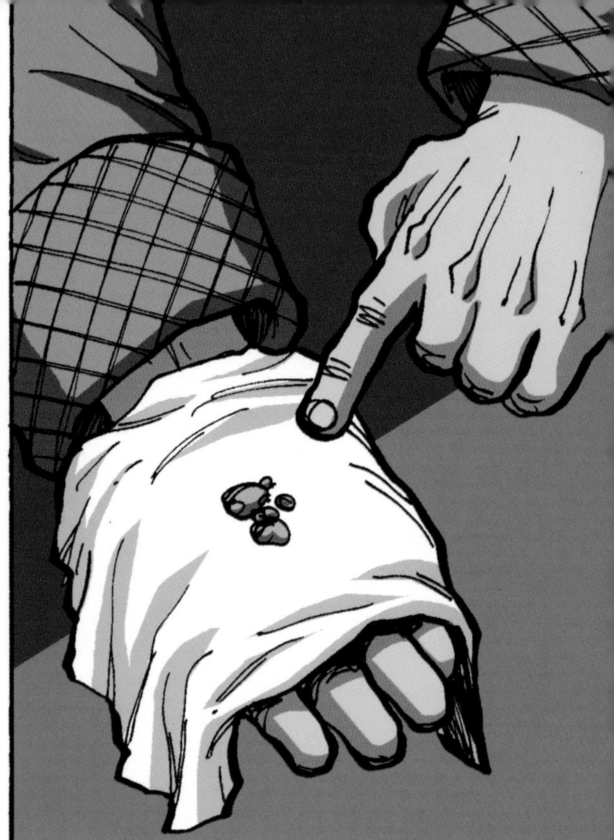

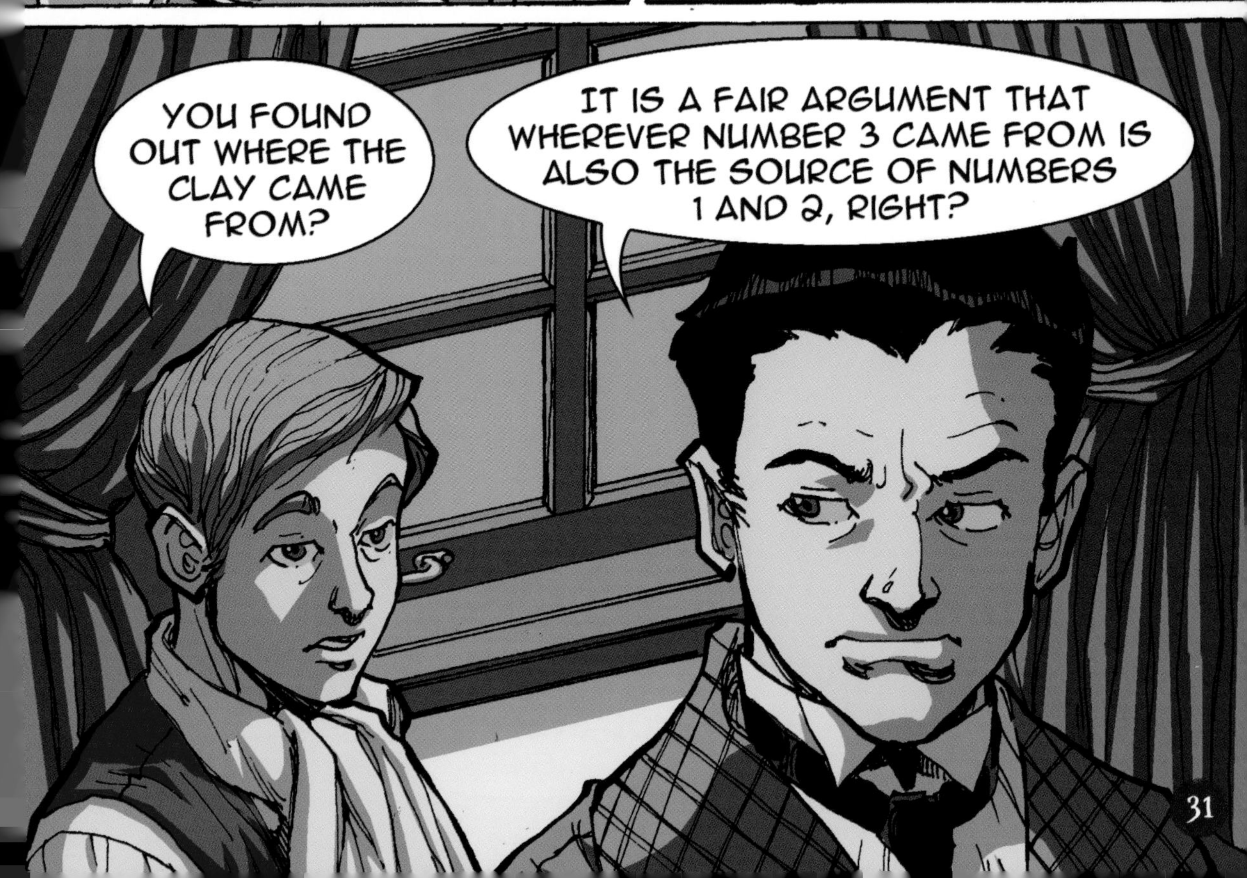
YOU FOUND OUT WHERE THE CLAY CAME FROM?
IT IS A FAIR ARGUMENT THAT WHEREVER NUMBER 3 CAME FROM IS ALSO THE SOURCE OF NUMBERS 1 AND 2, RIGHT?

THANK HEAVEN YOU CAME! I WAS WORRIED YOU HAD GIVEN UP.
WHAT AM I TO DO? SHALL THE EXAMINATION PROCEED?
BY ALL MEANS, YES. I HAVE FOUND THE RASCAL.
WHO WAS IT?
MR. BANNISTER, WILL YOU PLEASE TELL US THE TRUTH ABOUT YESTERDAY'S INCIDENT?
BANNISTER?! I'LL NOT BELIEVE IT.
I HAVE TOLD YOU EVERYTHING, SIR.

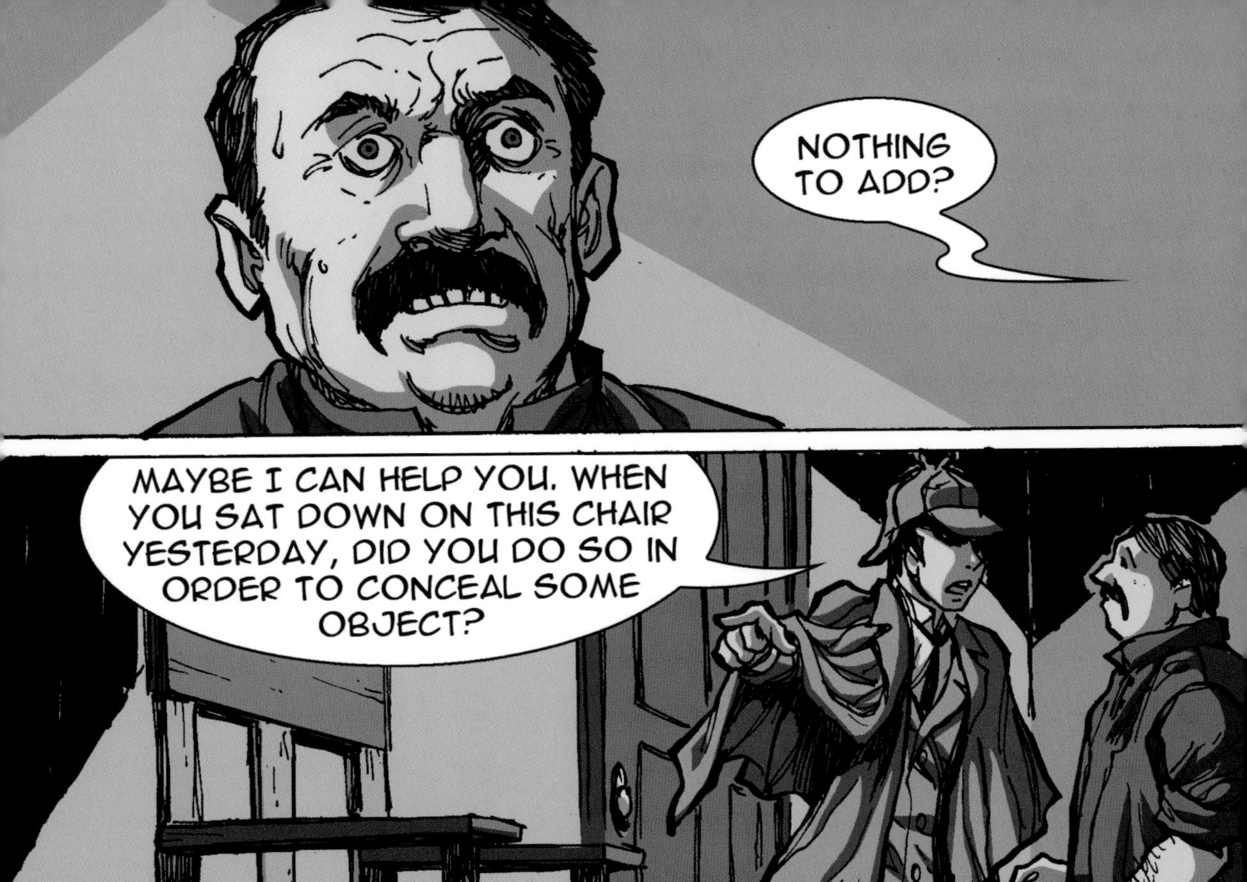
NOTHING TO ADD?
MAYBE I CAN HELP YOU. WHEN YOU SAT DOWN ON THIS CHAIR YESTERDAY, DID YOU DO SO IN ORDER TO CONCEAL SOME OBJECT?

CERTAINLY... CERTAINLY NOT.
I FRANKLY ADMIT, I AM UNABLE TO PROVE ANYTHING. BUT IT SEEMS PROBABLE THAT THE MOMENT MR. SOAMES'S BACK WAS TURNED, YOU RELEASED THE MAN WHO WAS HIDING IN THAT BEDROOM!
NO, SIR. THERE WAS NO ONE.

GOOD MORNING, MR. GILCHRIST.
I BROUGHT HIM, JUST AS YOU ASKED.
WHAT'S THIS ABOUT? I'D LIKE TO STUDY A BIT BEFORE THE EXAM.

WHAT I WOULD LIKE TO KNOW IS, HOW COULD AN HONORABLE MAN LIKE YOU COMMIT SUCH AN ACTION AS YOU DID YESTERDAY?

I NEVER SAID A WORD! NEVER A WORD!
BUT YOU HAVE NOW!

MR. GILCHRIST, WOULD YOU LIKE TO TELL ME WHAT HAPPENED?
OR PERHAPS IT WOULD BE EASIER FOR ME TO TELL MR. SOAMES. THEN, YOU CAN CORRECT ME WHERE I'M WRONG.
HOW HIGH IS THIS WINDOW? SEVEN FEET? I IMAGINE SOMEONE WHO WAS TALL AND COULD JUMP HIGH COULD SEE THE PAPERS SITTING IN YOUR OFFICE.

NOW IT JUST SO HAPPENED THAT THIS MAN SAW A KEY IN THE DOOR. A SUDDEN IMPULSE CAME OVER HIM TO ENTER AND SEE IF THE PAPERS WERE THE NEXT DAY'S TEST.
WHEN HE SAW IT WAS THE PASSAGE, HE PUT HIS SHOES ON THE DESK. MR. SOAMES, WHAT DO JUMPING SHOES LOOK LIKE?
THEY HAVE LONG METAL SPIKES.
THE CUTS ON THE DESK.

YOU'LL ALSO REMEMBER THAT THAT'S WHERE WE FOUND THE DIRT, THE EXACT SAME TYPE OF DIRT FOUND ON THE TRACK.
BRILLIANT!
MR. GILCHRIST, THERE IS ONE THING I KNOW I MISSED. WHAT DID YOU PUT ON THE CHAIR NEAR THE WINDOW?
GLOVES.
HE PUT HIS GLOVES ON THE CHAIR. AND HE TOOK THE PAPERS, SHEET BY SHEET, TO COPY THEM.

"WHEN YOU HEARD MR. SOAMES COMING, YOU RAN QUICKLY TO THE BEDROOM..."
"...AND FORGOT YOUR GLOVES."
HAVE I TOLD THE TRUTH, MR. GILCHRIST?
YES, YOU HAVE.

BUT I'M NO LONGER TAKING THE EXAMINATION. I HAVE BEEN OFFERED A COMMISSION IN THE RHODESIAN POLICE, AND I AM GOING TO SOUTH AFRICA AT ONCE.
I'M GLAD YOU'RE NOT GOING TO PROFIT FROM YOUR UNFAIR ADVANTAGE.
BUT WHY DID YOU CHOOSE TO NOT TAKE THE EXAMINATION?

BANNISTER CHANGED MY MIND.

A LONG TIME AGO, I WAS THE BUTLER TO GILCHRIST'S FATHER. WHEN THE FAMILY FELL INTO DEBT, THEY COULD NO LONGER AFFORD MY SERVICES. SO I STARTED WORKING HERE.
BUT I NEVER FORGOT MY OLD EMPLOYER. I WATCHED SIR JABEZ GILCHRIST'S SON WHILE I WAS HERE.

"WHEN I SAW MR. GILCHRIST'S TAN GLOVES LYING IN THAT CHAIR, I KNEW EXACTLY WHAT HAD HAPPENED."

"I FLOPPED DOWN INTO THAT CHAIR, AND NOTHING WOULD BUDGE ME UNTIL MR. SOAMES WENT FOR YOU."

"THEN MR. GILCHRIST CAME OUT OF THE BEDROOM AND CONFESSED IT ALL TO ME."
WASN'T IT NATURAL THAT I SHOULD PROTECT HIM FROM BEING EXPELLED? AND WASN'T IT NATURAL THAT I MAKE HIM UNDERSTAND HE COULD NOT PROFIT FROM SUCH A DEED? COULD YOU BLAME ME?
NO, INDEED.
WELL, MR. SOAMES, I HAVE CLEARED YOUR LITTLE PROBLEM.
FOR ME, BREAKFAST AWAITS. YOU HAVE A TEST TO GIVE.

THANK YOU, MR. GILCHRIST, FOR YOUR HONESTY. I TRUST A BRIGHT FUTURE AWAITS YOU IN RHODESIA.
The End

How to Draw Sherlock Holmes

by Ben Dunn

Step 1: Use a pencil to draw a simple framework. You can start with a stick figure! Then add circles, ovals, and cylinders to get the basic form. Getting the simple shapes in place is the beginning to solving any great case.

Step 2: Time to add to Sherlock's look. Use the shapes you started with to fill in his clothes. Use guidelines to add circles for the eyes. And don't forget the hair.

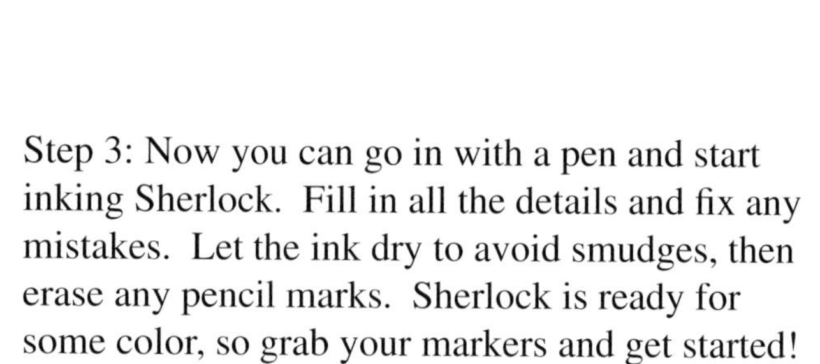

Step 3: Now you can go in with a pen and start inking Sherlock. Fill in all the details and fix any mistakes. Let the ink dry to avoid smudges, then erase any pencil marks. Sherlock is ready for some color, so grab your markers and get started!

Glossary

circumstances - conditions at a certain time or place.
collapsed - fell down.
culprit - a person guilty of something.
debt - something owed to someone, usually money.
dilemma - a difficult problem or decision.
discretion - careful to keep things quiet or private.
expelled - forced to leave.
expertise - the skill of someone who has a special knowledge of a subject.
incident - an event or happening that may form part of a larger event.
intriguing - something that causes great interest.
postpone - to put off until a later time.
scandal - an action that shocks people and disgraces those connected with it.
scholarship - money or aid given to help a student continue his or her studies.
suspicious - causing a feeling that something is wrong.
translate - the act of changing one language to another.
undisciplined - having no self-control.

Web Sites

To learn more about Sir Arthur Conan Doyle, visit ABDO Group online at **www.abdopublishing.com**. Web sites about Doyle are featured on our Book Links page. These links are routinely monitored and updated to provide the most current information available.

About the Author

Arthur Conan Doyle was born on May 22, 1859, in Edinburgh, Scotland. He was the second of Charles Altamont and Mary Foley Doyle's ten children. In 1868, Doyle began his schooling in England. Eight years later, he returned to Scotland.

Upon his return, Doyle entered the University of Edinburgh's medical school, where he became a doctor in 1885. That year, he married Louisa Hawkins. Together they had two children.

While a medical student, Doyle was impressed when his professor observed the tiniest details of a patient's condition. Doyle later wrote stories where his most famous character, Sherlock Holmes, used this same technique to solve mysteries. Holmes first appeared in *A Study in Scarlet* in 1887 and was immediately popular.

Between 1887 and 1927, Doyle wrote 66 stories and 3 novels about Holmes. He also wrote other fiction and nonfiction novels throughout his life. In 1902, Doyle was knighted for his work in a field hospital in the South African War. Four years later, Louisa died. Doyle married Jean Leckie in 1907, and they had three children together.

Sir Arthur Conan Doyle died on July 7, 1930, in Sussex, England. Today, Doyle's famous character, Sherlock Holmes, is honored with societies around the world that pay tribute to the detective.

Additional Works

A Study in Scarlet (1887)

The Mystery of Cloomber (1889)

The Firm of Girdlestone (1890)

The White Company (1891)

The Adventures of Sherlock Holmes (1891-92)

The Memoirs of Sherlock Holmes (1892-93)

Round the Red Lamp (1894)

The Stark Munro Letters (1895)

The Great Boer War (1900)

The Hound of the Baskervilles (1901-02)

The Return of Sherlock Holmes (1903-04)

Through the Magic Door (1907)

The Crime of the Congo (1909)

The Coming of the Fairies (1922)

Memories and Adventures (1924)

The Case-Book of Sherlock Holmes (1921-27)

About the Adapters

Author

Vincent Goodwin earned his BA in Drama and Communications from Trinity University in San Antonio. He is the writer of three plays as well as the cowriter of the comic book *Pirates vs. Ninjas II*. Goodwin is also an accomplished journalist, having won several awards for his work as a columnist and reporter.

Illustrator

Ben Dunn founded Antarctic Press, one of the largest comic companies in the United States. His works appear in Marvel and Image comics. He is best known for his series *Ninja High School* and *Warrior Nun Areala*.